What
If
Elephants
Wore
Hula
Skirts?

by Joy Au

illustrations by
Al Furtado

MUTUAL

First Printing,
September 1997

1 2 3 4 5 6 7 8 9

ISBN 1-56647-150-8

Mutual Publishing
1127 11th Avenue, Mezz. B
Honolulu, Hawaii 96816
Telephone (808) 732-1709
Fax (808) 734-4094
e-mail: mutual@lava.net

Printed in Taiwan

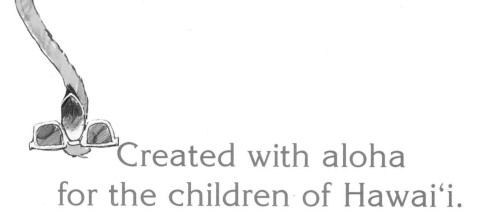

Created with aloha
for the children of Hawai'i.

Mahalo nui loa to
Alfred, Bennett, Gay, Jane, Betsy,
Kei, Marylou, Richard, Sean,
Jeanine, Alma, Ken, Geof, & Maile
for believing that dreams
can come true.

What if elephants wore hula skirts...

Would they dance by the light of the moon?

And, if hippos surfed big waves...

Would they hang-ten and shoot-the-tube?

What if bears jitter-bugged in Jams...

Would they cause traffic to stop?

And, if monkeys went windsurfing...

Would they sail away to Bombay?

What if alligators played ukuleles...

Would the tigers join in with kazoos?

And, if lions pulled rickshaws...

INTERNATIONAL MARKETPLACE

ALOHA

Would peacocks go for a ride or run along side?

What if giraffes ate chocolate chip cookies...

Would they drink some milk to wash it down?

And if camels dressed aloha style...

Would they sip ice tea under a banyan tree?

What if flamingos stayed at a pink hotel...

Would you be able to see them very well?

And, if porcupines went parasailing...

Would they eat pumpkin pie in the sky?

What if zebras got a suntan...

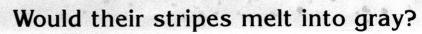

Would their stripes melt into gray?

And, if tortoises went for a romantic cruise...

Would they hug and kiss or take a snooze?

What if all the animials celebrated a baby luau...
With slack key music and good kau kau?
Well, they just might at the Honolulu Zoo.
And, YOU CAN join their party, too!

See you at the zoo!

GLOSSARY

Alligator
Alligator fish for their food by slapping the water to scare their prey. Sometimes, they cruise under water and pounce on their prey who cannot see them until it is too late.

Bear
Bears eat lots of berries, fruits, roots, insects and some meat to prepare for the winter. They do not hibernate during the winter and sometimes will come out to play on warm winter days.

Camel
A dromedary is a camel with one hump and a bactrian is a camel with two humps. A baby camel is a foal.

Elephant
Elephants are not afraid of mice. A mother elephant will carry her baby for 22 months. Baby elephants will stay with their mothers for 14 years.

Flamingo
Holding their bills upside down in the water, flamingos eat tiny water plants and animals. Flamingos live in flocks.

Giraffe
Giraffes can stretch their necks to eat the best leaves in a tall tree that other animals cannot reach. Baby giraffes are born at about 6 feet tall.

Hippo
Although hippopotamuses can run faster than the fastest human, they like to hang-out in the water all day. Baby hippos can weigh 100 pounds.

Lion
Male lions have long hair growing around their necks called manes. Female lions do not have manes. Lions live in family groups called prides on the grassy African Savanna.

Monkey
Monkeys spend most of their lives in trees. Like humans, mother monkeys take special care of their babies. Monkeys live in troops and spend hours cleaning each other.

Peacock
Male peacocks strut and fan their tails in order to get female peahens to look at them.

Porcupine
Porcupines have about 30,000 quills on its body. Baby porcupines are born with soft quills that harden in a few hours.

Tiger
The stripes on tigers camouflage them in tall grass. Tigers are not hesitant about getting wet and may go for a swim. Tiger mothers may have one to three cubs in a litter.

Tortoise
Tortoises can weigh 700 pounds and live a long life of up to 100 years.

Zebra
A relative of the horse, zebras live in herds on the plains of Africa. Mother zebras usually have one foal. Each zebra is born with its own pattern of stripes.